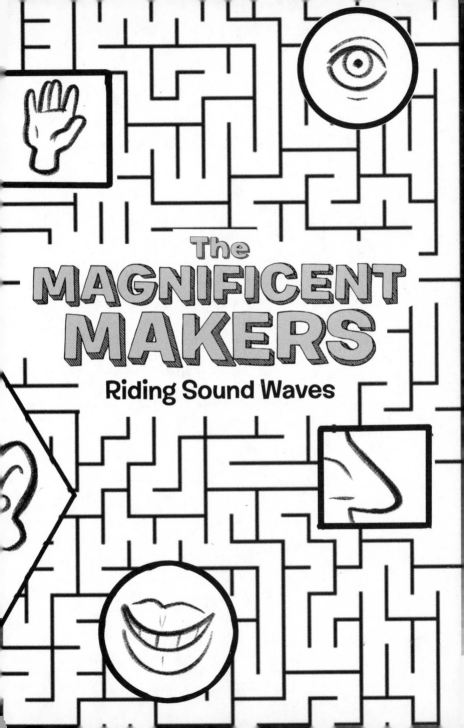

The
MAGNIFICENT
MAKERS

Riding Sound Waves

Go on more
a-MAZE-ing adventures with

The
MAGNIFICENT
MAKERS

How to Test a Friendship

Brain Trouble

Riding Sound Waves

The MAGNIFICENT MAKERS

3

Riding Sound Waves

by Theanne Griffith
illustrated by Reggie Brown

A STEPPING STONE BOOK™
Random House New York

Text copyright © 2020 by Theanne Griffith
Cover art and interior illustrations copyright © 2020 by Reginald Brown

Visit us on the Web!
rhcbooks.com

Educators and librarians, for a variety of teaching tools, visit us at
RHTeachersLibrarians.com

Library of Congress Cataloging-in-Publication Data
Names: Griffith, Theanne, author. | Brown, Reggie, illustrator.
Title: Riding sound waves / by Theanne Griffith;
illustrations by Reggie Brown.
Description: First edition. | New York: Random House Children's Books, [2020] | Series: The Magnificent Makers; 3 | "A Stepping Stone book." | Audience: Ages 7–10. | Summary: "In the Maker Maze—a magical makerspace—Violet and Pablo, along with their classmate Henry, learn all about the senses and how different people might experience them."—Provided by publisher
Identifiers: LCCN 2019048039 (print) | LCCN 2019048040 (ebook) | ISBN 978-0-593-12310-2 (trade pbk.) | ISBN 978-0-593-12311-9 (library binding) | ISBN 978-0-593-12312-6 (ebook)
Subjects: CYAC: Senses and sensation—Fiction. | Makerspaces—Fiction. | People with disabilities—Fiction. | Friendship—Fiction.
Classification: LCC PZ7.1.G7527 Rid 2020 (print) | LCC PZ7.1.G7527 (ebook) | DDC [Fic]—dc23

Printed in the United States of America
10 9 8 7 6 5 4 3 2 1

First Edition

This book has been officially leveled by using
the F&P Text Level Gradient™ Leveling System.

Random House Children's Books supports the
First Amendment and celebrates the right to read.

To all those who see
Henry in themselves
—T.G.

To my brothers, Craig and Jay.
I'm without a doubt the favorite now.
—R.B.

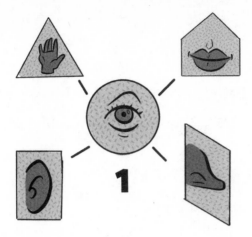

*S*creeeeeeeeeech!

The Newburg Elementary school bus came to a sudden stop. Pablo and Violet lunged forward.

"I thought we'd never get here," Pablo moaned as he stretched his arms overhead. The two best friends unfastened their seat belts and looked out the window. Cars, buses, and taxis honked as they zoomed through the streets. People scurried down steps to catch the subway. The smell of hot dogs started to fill the

bus. They had finally arrived in the city.
Next stop, the City Science Museum!

"Can we get off yet?" Violet bounced in
her seat.

"Hopefully," said Pablo. "I haven't been
here since last year."

"Me neither. Remember how we learned about viruses? And how fast they can travel around the world?" asked Violet.

"Yeah," said Pablo. "I wonder what we'll get to see this year."

Pablo and Violet weren't the only ones who were excited. The bus hummed with the voices of Mr. Eng's third-grade class. This was the first field trip of the year, and everyone had been on the bus for more than an hour.

Mr. Eng stood up from the first row and raised his hand to quiet everyone.

"Okay, class," he began. "Time to buddy up. Remember the double line we practiced?"

"Yes, Mr. Eng!" answered the class.

Pablo and Violet were always field trip buddies. In fact, they did everything together. At recess, they either played soccer or double Dutch. And they always shared a sweet, juicy pickle from the Newburg Corner Store on their walk home from school. Recently, Pablo had started helping Violet learn Spanish. And they both loved everything about science. Pablo dreamt of being an astronaut and traveling through space. Violet was determined to become a scientist and cure as many diseases as possible.

"Listo?" said Violet. "Are you ready?"

"Muy bien!" replied Pablo. The Spanish lessons were working. He grabbed his best friend's hand, and they peeled their legs from the sticky seats.

"Come on, Henry!" Violet called toward the back of the bus. A boy wearing a tight-fitting black-and-green superhero costume sat in the last row. Two blue eyes gazed over the seats from behind a silver mask.

"New costume?" Pablo asked with a smile as Henry made his way to the front.

"Yeah!" replied Henry. "My other one got a hole in the armpit."

There was an odd number of students in the class, so Mr. Eng added Henry to Violet and Pablo's group. Pablo always tried to be nice to Henry, who was a little different from other kids. Sometimes he would throw tantrums for no reason at all, especially during gym or recess. And he could never sit still and pay attention in class. But Pablo knew what it was like to be different. He had felt different from his classmates when he'd first arrived in Newburg from Puerto Rico. Luckily, he'd met Violet. She thought his differences were cool.

"It's time to take off your mask now,"
Mr. Eng said to Henry as they hopped off
the bus.

Henry held the sides of his mask with
both hands.

Mr. Eng knelt down. "I know you like
wearing your mask. But the rules for entering the museum are the same as the rules
for entering school. No hats," he said. "Or
masks."

Henry's hands didn't budge.

"Please?" asked Mr. Eng.

Henry sighed and slowly removed the mask. He shook out his wavy blond hair as he gave the mask to Mr. Eng.

"Thank you." Mr. Eng smiled.

"It's so loud out here," Henry complained, covering his ears.

Violet smiled and grabbed Pablo's and Henry's hands. "Come on, then! Let's go," she said. The trio hurried inside.

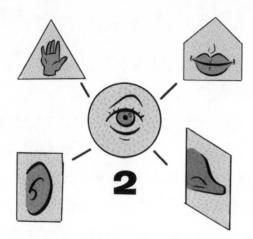

2

"**R**oar!" growled Violet. She held up her hands, imitating the towering T. rex standing in the middle of the museum lobby.

Henry jumped. "Hey! Don't do that." He frowned. "You scared me."

"Sorry, I didn't mean to," replied Violet.

"Yeah, she was just joking around," said Pablo.

"Okay . . . but . . . it's loud enough in here," said Henry. The building was huge, with high ceilings and tall stone columns.

Laughter and screams echoed from the planetarium on the second floor.

Mr. Eng removed a pencil from behind his ear and waved it in the air. Then he pointed to a brightly colored section of the museum with various rooms waiting to be explored. "Today in the Kids' Corner, you're going to learn all about our five senses. Can anyone remind the class what they are?"

Pablo's and Violet's hands shot into the air.

Mr. Eng called on Violet.

"Hearing, taste, smell, sight, and . . ." She forgot the last one.

"Touch!" added Pablo.

"Great job!" said Mr. Eng. "Now, who's ready to have some fun?"

"We are!" the class cheered, and then scattered.

"Vamos!" said Pablo. He ran toward a room with a giant eye painted on the door. Violet and Henry followed.

"Whoa!" said the trio as soon as they entered. The room was white with black lines drawn all over it. Even the floor was covered with lines that swirled and twisted.

"It looks like the walls are curved," said Pablo, reaching out his hand. "But they're not. They're flat!"

"This is so weird. I think my eyes are confused!" said Violet with her arms stretched out to her sides.

"I'm getting dizzy," said Henry as he wobbled around.

"Me too," said Pablo.

The buddies slowly wandered back out into the lobby. Henry covered his ears. "Let's find a new room," he said.

"Look over there!" Pablo pointed to a door with a giant nose hanging over it.

"I hope that thing doesn't have boogers!" said Violet, scrunching up her face.

"Gross!" Henry said, pulling on the sleeves of his costume.

WORLD OF
SMELL

"Better hurry! Don't want any snot falling on you!" said Pablo.

They were greeted with a sweet smell as they entered.

"Mmmmm," said Violet, rubbing her belly. "It smells like—"

"CAKE!" Pablo blurted out.

He pointed to the middle of the room,

where a three-layered chocolate cake sat on a stand inside a clear glass box. Colorful noses made of icing decorated each layer. There were cards hanging from plastic cords on a bar that surrounded the stand.

"They're scratch-and-sniff!" Henry said, holding a card in his hand. "It says here that each card smells like an ingredient used to make the cake."

Violet scratched one and sniffed. "Eeeew! This smells nasty! If the cake tastes like *this,* then I don't want any." She let the card drop.

Henry picked it up. "Yuck!" He pinched his nose. "Smells like vinegar."

Pablo examined the next card. Just as he was about to sniff, he noticed a riddle written on the back.

"Violet, look!" Pablo's voice squeaked with excitement. "I think it's from Dr. Crisp!"

"Who's Dr. Crisp?" asked Henry.

"Oh, she's just the coolest scientist *ever*!" replied Violet.

"And she runs the Maker Maze," Pablo explained. "It's this magical makerspace."

Henry's face lit up. "Really?"

Violet tucked her wild, curly hair behind her ears. "Yup. And we get there through a portal of purple light. But we have to answer this riddle first."

She read it aloud:

BAKING A CAKE ISN'T HARD TO DO.
YOU JUST NEED A FEW INGREDIENTS,
AND A PAN OR TWO.
USE YOUR SENSE OF _____
TO MEASURE JUST RIGHT.
FEEL THE BATTER,
USING YOUR SENSE OF _____.
IT MIGHT BE YUMMY,
BUT DON'T EAT TOO MUCH!
WHEN IT'S ALMOST READY, YOU'LL KNOW!
YOUR SENSE OF _____ WILL TELL YOU SO.
BUT WHEN IT'S ACTUALLY TIME,
YOU'LL _____ THE OVEN BELL CHIME.
HURRY, HURRY, THERE'S NO TIME TO WASTE!
TRY THE CAKE USING YOUR SENSE OF_____!

Violet bit her lip. "Well, the last one is obvious," she said. "Taste!"

"And you *hear* a bell chime," added Pablo.

"Henry, do you think . . . ," Violet began. But Henry wasn't paying attention. He was over by the door, looking into the giant nose.

"Hey, Henry! Come back," Pablo called across the room.

"Don't yell at me!" said Henry. His eyebrows squished together.

Pablo glanced at Violet. "Uh . . . I was just trying to get your attention," he said. "We need to figure this out."

Henry fiddled with his costume sleeve and walked back over to the group.

"You feel by touching," continued Violet.

"What about the other two?" asked Pablo.

Henry shrugged. "I don't like riddles," he said. "They're confusing."

Violet bit her lip. "I think the first one is sight!"

"Sounds right. And you start to smell a cake when it's almost done!" added Pablo.

Suddenly, everything in the room

began to shake! The scratch-and-sniff cards danced along the bar.

"What's going on?" said Henry. His voice trembled with the rest of the room.

BOOM! SNAP! WHIZ! ZAP!

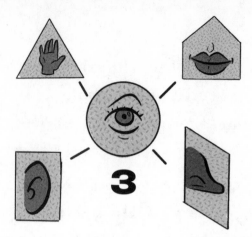

"**A**re you okay?" asked Pablo. Henry was crouched on the floor with his hands over his ears.

Violet tapped Henry on the shoulder. He looked at Pablo and Violet and slowly lowered his hands. He stood up and crossed his arms. "What *was* that?" he asked.

"It was the portal. It opened," Violet replied.

"It sounded like the portal exploded," said Henry as he fixed his costume.

Pablo and Violet giggled. Then Pablo saw a purple light near the door. "This way!" he said, rushing out of the room.

"What happened to everyone?" asked Henry.

Their classmates were scattered throughout the Kids' Corner. But they weren't moving. Smiles were stuck on the students' faces.

"Time stops when the portal opens," explained Violet. "Look at Deepak!" She pointed to one of their classmates. He was frozen in the air! It looked like the spaceships on his sneakers were blasting him into space.

Pablo smiled as he tapped Violet on the shoulder.

"No way! We have to enter through

there?" asked Violet. She shivered. "Not cool, Dr. Crisp."

The giant nose hanging over the door was glowing within a ring of purple light.

Pablo laughed. "Look at your hair!"

Violet's curls were sticking straight up! She giggled. "Your hair's doing it, too, Henry!"

"It must be the portal," said Pablo. He patted his head. "My hair is too short."

"I think it will suck us up if we jump high enough," Violet said, biting her lip.

"Will the portal make that exploding noise again when we go through it?" asked Henry nervously.

"No," replied Violet. She thought for a moment. "But it will feel like a hug that tingles."

"Ready?" asked Pablo. The trio joined hands and squatted before leaping into the air.

BIZZAP!

Pablo, Violet, and Henry landed on the floor of the Maker Maze. They dusted themselves off and stood up.

"This is even cooler than I imagined!" said Henry.

Pablo and Violet gave Henry a tour of the main lab. They showed Henry the robots that were unpacking a box of supplies near the huge microscope. They walked between the long tables, where colorful liquids bubbled in flasks and strange plants jiggled and danced.

"What's that?" asked Henry, pushing his face against a giant glass jar. Inside, a blue three-winged beetle flew in circles.

"No idea," replied Pablo. "But these are my favorite!" He pointed to the floating crystals in the zero gravity chambers.

"Dr. Crisp, we're here!" Violet shouted down a long hallway lined with doors.

"We go through one of those doors to start the challenge," explained Pablo.

Then a voice behind them said, "Well, hello, Makers!"

The trio turned around. Dr. Crisp stood tall with her wild rainbow hair and bright purple pants. The Maker Manual was tucked under her arm. A name tag was fastened to her white lab coat.

"Lovely seeing you two, as always." She winked at Pablo and Violet. "And nice to meet you, Henry! Cool outfit!"

"You know my name?" said Henry with a big smile. He stood proudly in his costume.

"Of course!" she replied.

"Is that your special power? Are you a superhero?" asked Henry.

Dr. Crisp laughed. "Superhero, no. Super-scientist, YES!" She put her fists on her hips and puffed out her chest.

Henry looked at his feet and tugged on the sleeves of his costume. "What else do you know about me?" he asked.

Dr. Crisp tapped her chin with her fingers. "I know the Maker Maze thought you'd be the perfect person to help Pablo and Violet today!" She took the Maker Manual from under her arm. It snapped open to a page with the day of the week at the top. Below were pictures of Pablo, Violet, and Henry! "You see?" She pointed with her pencil to the name under each picture.

"Since we have the book open," Pablo said, "let's start the challenge!"

"Yeah!" agreed Violet.

Dr. Crisp flipped the pages of the glittery golden book to one with a large question mark. She explained the rules to Henry. "All you have to do is tell the Maker Manual what you want to learn about today. The Maze will design a challenge with three different levels. You'll have one hundred twenty Maker Minutes to finish, and—"

"Henry! This is important," said Pablo.

Henry had wandered toward the robots.

"We only have one hundred twenty Maker Minutes to get back to the museum before everyone unfreezes." Pablo pointed to the screen above them. It showed the Kids' Corner, where the students were as still as the T. rex.

Henry blushed as he walked back over to the group.

"Sorry," he said.

"That's all right." Dr. Crisp smiled. "Sometimes I get distracted by the cool stuff in the Maze, too." She tapped the Maker Manual with her pencil. "So, Makers, what's today's science topic?"

Pablo and Violet said together, "Let's learn about our senses!"

The pages of the Maker Manual began to turn slowly but quickly gained speed. Then they suddenly stopped. The page read:

LEVEL 1: MYSTERY MAKER BOX

Go to door number one to begin.

Dr. Crisp closed the Maker Manual and stuffed it in a backpack lying by her feet. Pablo, Violet, and Henry felt something on their wrists.

"Our Magnificent Maker Watches!" Pablo said.

"We need them to keep track of Maker Minutes," Violet explained to Henry. "We can only come back if we finish in time."

"Okay, Makers! Let's get a move on!" Dr. Crisp did three cartwheels and a backflip. She landed in front of door number one. Pablo, Violet, and Henry rushed behind her. As she opened the door, their watches glowed and vibrated.

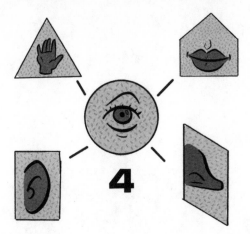

4

The room was pitch-black. All the Makers could hear was the sound of one another's breathing. Suddenly, Dr. Crisp's voice boomed over a loudspeaker.

"Step right up, step right up, Makers! Welcome to the first level of your sensory adventure!"

Henry frowned as he covered his ears.

The lights flashed on, and the room glowed purple. Wide streamers and banners draped the ceiling. Colorful, confetti-filled balloons floated through

the air. They were tied into different animal shapes. At the far end of the room, Dr. Crisp stood on a stage in the middle of a spotlight. Next to her was a large black box with a purple *M* painted on the side.

"This is a circus," said Henry, pulling on his sleeve. "Not a makerspace." A giant llama balloon floated over his head. "I don't know if I like it."

"Don't worry, I'm sure you're going to love it!" said Violet with a smile. She darted toward the stage. Pablo and Henry hurried after her.

"In this level, we are going to explore our sense of touch," said Dr. Crisp, tapping her pointer fingers together. "And we'll be using this Mystery Maker Box!" She gave the box a slap.

"How does it work?" Pablo asked.

"This box is full of all kinds of goodies," Dr. Crisp began.

"Like candy?" asked Henry.

"Not this time." Dr. Crisp laughed. Then she pointed to a hole in the top of the box. "In the first part of the level, you'll stick your hands in here and dig around. When you grab something, you'll have to guess what it is. But you can *only* use your hands. No peeking! And you have to guess correctly before you take the item out of the box."

Dr. Crisp opened her backpack. "Here are your Mystery Mittens!" she said, tossing each Maker a pair. "In the second part, you're going to guess what you grab while wearing these. You might notice . . . a difference." Dr. Crisp winked. "To complete the level, you'll have to figure out why it's so different exploring the Mystery Maker Box with mittens on."

"There isn't anything in there that can hurt us, right?" asked Henry, peering through the dark opening.

"Most definitely not!" replied Dr. Crisp. She held up her right hand with her three middle fingers down, making an *M*. "Maker's honor." Then she pressed a button on the side of her watch. "Activate Mystery Maker Box!" The watch glowed purple. "Ready, set, DIG!"

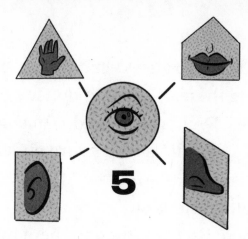

Violet went first. She reached into the box with both hands and fumbled around. Eventually, she grabbed something. She ran her hands along the object's curves and edges. Suddenly, her eyes grew wide and a smile flashed on her face.

"No way! It's a microscope!"

RING, DING, DONG!

Violet lifted a bright purple mini-microscope from the box.

"It matches your pants, Dr. Crisp!" Pablo pointed out.

"Purple happens to be my favorite color," said Dr. Crisp, strutting around the stage. Everyone laughed.

"Can I go next?" asked Henry.

"Sure!" replied Pablo and Violet.

Henry reached in. "I got something!" he said. He pulled his arms out. But his hands were empty.

"Ah, ah, ah! You have to guess what you're holding *before* you pull it out of the box. If you don't, it will disappear," said Dr. Crisp with a snap of her fingers.

"She told us that already," said Pablo. "Remember?"

"I know!" Henry frowned. "I just got . . . confused." His cheeks turned pink as he reached back in. He grabbed something else and traced it with his fingertips.

"This has to be a belt!" he said after a few moments.

RING, DING, DONG!

Henry pulled out a green belt with a shiny black buckle. An *H* was drawn on it.

"It matches my costume!" said Henry.

"Now we just need to get you a cape!" cheered Dr. Crisp.

Pablo went last. After digging for a while, he got his hands on something. It felt just like . . .

"A spaceship!" shouted Pablo, holding it high in the air. It was exactly like the ones on his sneakers.

"Now it's time to mitten up," said Dr. Crisp.

"I wonder if they'll help us feel the objects better," said Pablo. He examined the Mystery Mittens carefully.

"Can I go first this time?" Henry asked.

"Go ahead!" replied Violet.

Henry reached into the Mystery Maker Box. "Whoa, this *is* different," he said.

"What do you mean?" asked Pablo.

"Well, I can kind of feel stuff. But it's

hard to tell what anything is." Henry kept digging. "I think I have a . . . stick?" When he pulled his hands out of the box, they were empty.

"Are you sure you put the Mystery Mittens on right, Henry?" asked Pablo.

Henry's shoulders became tense. "I know how to put on mittens! I learned how to do that when I was, like, four," he replied.

"It's just that . . . sometimes you have trouble with directions," Pablo continued.

"Why don't you give it a try, then? You'll see it's not so easy," Henry said to Pablo.

Pablo reached in and felt around for a minute. "I can't tell what anything is!" He sighed.

"Told you," Henry mumbled.

"Let me try," said Violet. But she didn't have any luck, either.

"I think we need to stop," said Pablo. "Otherwise we're going to run out of time."

"Okay, let's solve the level," said Violet, taking off her mittens.

Pablo scratched his cheek. "It's weird. I mean, I could feel stuff in the box when I had the mittens on."

"Yeah," agreed Violet. "I knew I had grabbed something. I could kind of figure out its shape. But I couldn't actually tell *what* it was. What about you, Henry?"

Henry was staring off into space.

"Henry?" said Pablo.

Henry jumped. "What?" he replied with a frown.

"We need your help," Pablo replied. He pointed at his watch.

"Um, I'm thinking." Henry paused. "What was the question, again?"

"Henry, please," said Pablo. "You've got to pay attention."

"I'm trying my best," said Henry.

"Wait a minute!" said Violet. "I think I have an idea. What about our skin!"

"Huh?" said Pablo.

"The mittens. We put them on our *hands*, but they're also covering our *skin*!" Violet wiggled her fingers.

"I think you're right!" said Henry, jumping up and down. "It's like trying to tie your shoes in the winter with gloves on! It's so much harder when you can't really feel the laces."

"That's true!" Pablo agreed.

"Our skin must be important for our sense of touch!" said Violet.

RING, DING, DONG!

"Yes!" the trio cheered.

"I've got to *hand* it to you, Makers,"

said Dr. Crisp, pulling a purple ball out of the pocket in her lab coat. "You knocked that one out of the park!" She swung the microphone stand, sending the ball soaring through the air. Then she pulled the Maker Manual out of her backpack. It snapped open to a page that read:

LEVEL 2: GOING, GOING, GONG!

Swipe left.

Dr. Crisp tapped the screen of her watch three times and swiped left.

BIZZAP!

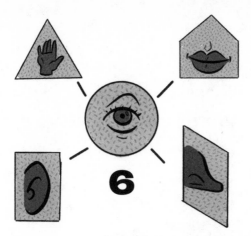

6

The stage, balloons, banners, and purple lights glided away. The Makers and Dr. Crisp were now standing in an empty room.

"Whoa!" said Henry. "How did you do that? Are you sure you don't have super-powers?" he asked Dr. Crisp through squinted eyes.

"Science is my superpower!" Dr. Crisp raised her fist in the air. Then she cupped her hands around her mouth and yelled, "Incoming!"

BIZZAP!

The Makers jumped out of the way as a large green bowl dropped from the ceiling. It landed with a thud. The bowl was huge!

"Where did that come from?" asked Pablo, searching the ceiling with his eyes.

"Secret door number six," replied Dr. Crisp. "Now listen closely, Makers!" She bent down and cupped a hand around one of her ears. "This level is all about hearing."

Violet smiled with her head tilted to the side. "I thought we were going to cook something. Like maybe a chocolate cake," she said. "And then *taste* it."

Dr. Crisp laughed. "Sorry to burst your Bunsen burner. No tasting in this level." Then she opened her backpack and started pulling out a long roll of plastic wrap.

"Stand back, Makers!" she grunted. After a few pulls, she finally got the whole thing out. It was even wider than the

bowl! Then she pulled out a giant jar of jelly beans and a huge rubber band.

"Uh-oh," said Pablo, giggling. "The bands are back!"

"I'm telling you, I need one of those backpacks!" added Violet.

Dr. Crisp explained the level. "Inside each ear, you have a tiny flap of skin called an eardrum."

"We have drums in our ears?" asked Henry, pulling on his costume sleeve. "That explains why it gets so noisy sometimes."

Dr. Crisp laughed. "Your eardrum isn't *that* kind of drum. But after this level, you'll understand how it got its name. You're going to make a model eardrum and then test it. To complete the level, you'll have to figure out how the eardrum detects sound."

Dr. Crisp opened the Maker Manual to a page with a list of instructions. Then she raised both arms overhead. As she lowered them, she shouted, "Ready, set, MAKE!"

First the Makers tore off a long piece of plastic wrap. Then they pulled the plastic tight and stretched it over the bowl.

"Now all we have to do is fasten it with a

rubber band," said Violet as she ran down the list of instructions with her finger.

Pablo, Violet, and Henry each grabbed a side of the band.

"Pull!" said Violet.

The Makers stretched the band with all their might.

"I think it's wide enough," said Pablo. Drops of sweat dotted his forehead.

Violet's arms trembled. "Let's hurry!"

"I'm not sure I can hold on much longer!" Pablo yelped. Just then, the band slipped from one of his hands.

"Hold tight, Henry!" called Violet.

"I'm trying!" he replied.

Pablo wiped his forehead with his free hand. "Okay, got it," he said.

The Makers carefully lifted and lowered the band around the bowl and plastic wrap.

"Let go on three!" shouted Violet. "One, two, THREE!"

SNAP!

RING, DING, DONG!

"Yeah!" The Makers celebrated with double high fives.

"Well, polish my pipette!" cheered Dr. Crisp. "Excellent teamwork!" She leaned on the bowl with her elbow and gave it a pat. "Now it's time to try this beauty out!" Dr. Crisp shouted into her watch. "Maker Maze, activate Going, Going, Gong!"

The floor began to shake. Pablo and Violet smiled, but Henry turned as white as a ghost.

"No, no, no!" he said as he raised his hands to his ears.

BOOM! SNAP! WHIZ! ZAP!

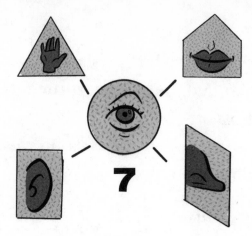

7

A bright purple light flashed through the room. When it faded, Pablo, Violet, and Dr. Crisp saw Henry balled up on the floor in the corner. His arms were folded over his head. Next to him stood a giant golden gong.

Dr. Crisp rushed over and leaned down. "Are you okay, Henry?" she asked. Her eyes were soft and her voice was gentle. Henry uncovered his head. His face was as red as a beet.

Pablo and Violet ran over, too.

"What happened?" asked Violet.

Pablo knelt next to Henry and placed a hand on his shoulder. "It's just a gong." Pablo smiled. "Don't worry. The Maker Maze is safe. Nothing here can hurt you. Right, Dr. Crisp?"

But before Dr. Crisp could respond, Henry stood up, stomped his feet, and let out a loud scream. "Just leave me alone!"

"But, Henry. We only want to make sure you're okay," said Violet.

"Why is everyone yelling at me? It's not my fault the Maze keeps exploding! Just let me be!" Henry replied with his hands over his ears. He started speed walking around the room.

Everyone got quiet. Pablo and Violet didn't know what to do. Even Dr. Crisp looked confused. After a few moments, Henry stopped. He took several deep breaths. Pablo glanced down at his watch. They didn't have much time.

"Henry?" said Pablo.

Henry opened his eyes but didn't move his hands.

"It's okay if you got scared. We all get scared sometimes," said Pablo.

Henry took another deep breath before lowering his hands. "I'm not scared," he finally said. The redness had faded from his face. "It's just that . . ." Henry fiddled with his fingers. Then he shook his head. "Never mind. It's nothing."

"Are you sure?" asked Violet. "Something really seems to be bothering you. You can tell us."

"Henry, you don't have to—" began Dr. Crisp.

But before she could finish, Henry made an *M* with his fingers and said, "I'm okay. Maker's honor." He smiled.

Dr. Crisp returned his smile and said, "Well, all righty then. Let's regroup." She walked around the gong as she explained the second half of level two.

Dr. Crisp raised a finger in the air. "Step one! Throw a handful of jelly beans on top of your model eardrum. Step two!" she shouted, raising a second finger. "One of you will strike the gong with this." Dr. Crisp pulled a golden mallet out of her lab coat pocket. It gleamed as she held it in the air.

Pablo jumped up and down with his hand raised. "Can I hit the gong?"

"You bet, space cadet!" replied Dr. Crisp. She tossed him the mallet.

"It looks like a magic wand!" said Violet.

Pablo waved it in the air. "*Abracadabra! Spaceship, appear!*"

"I want my own lab coat, just like Dr. Crisp!" Violet laughed.

Henry tugged on his sleeves and said, "I want the power to fly!"

"Your wish is my command!" said Pablo, waving the mallet at Violet and Henry.

Dr. Crisp continued. "Step three! Observe the model eardrum and jelly beans. And finally, step four! Decide how our eardrums hear sound," she said, flicking her ears with her fingers. Then she said, "No time to waste, Makers! Let's get *gong*ing!"

Dr. Crisp opened the giant jar and pushed it over. "Go ahead and grab a handful!" she said to Henry.

He reached in and tossed a bunch on top of the plastic.

Then Violet called to Pablo, "Ready when you are!"

"Wait!" yelled Henry.

Pablo tapped the mallet on the palm of his hand. "We have to hurry. We only have

50 min. left

fifty Maker Minutes left," he said with his wrist in the air.

Henry gulped as he looked back and forth between Pablo and the gong. "I think you should hit the gong softly," he said.

"Why?" asked Violet.

"Well, we don't want to break the eardrum, right?" said Henry.

"I don't think that's going to work," said Pablo, shaking his head.

"You never know until you try!" said Dr. Crisp. "Let's do an experiment and see!"

Pablo sighed and tapped the gong lightly with the mallet. A soft sound rippled through the room. Violet and Henry watched the jelly beans carefully.

Violet bit her lip. "I didn't see anything, did you?"

"No," Henry replied. "Maybe we made a mistake when we made the eardrum."

"There's nothing wrong with the eardrum," Pablo insisted. "We're wasting time. If we don't hurry and finish, we won't be able to come back!" He lifted the

mallet high over his head and crashed it into the gong as hard as he could.

GOOOOOOOOOOOOOOOOOOOONG!

Sound flooded the room. Suddenly, the jelly beans started dancing on the plastic!

"Wow! Look at them go!" said Violet.

But Henry couldn't see anything. With his hands over his ears, he shook his head as tears poured down his cheeks.

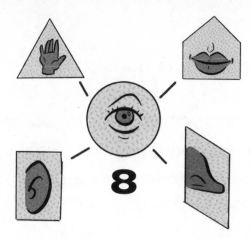

Pablo dropped the mallet and grabbed the gong with his hands. He squeezed tightly. Eventually, the ringing stopped and the jelly beans were still again. He ran over to the model eardrum. Dr. Crisp followed him.

"I'm . . . I'm sorry," said Pablo. "I didn't mean to hurt your feelings."

Henry was breathing so quickly it almost sounded like he was gasping for air. "You didn't hurt my feelings," he replied between breaths. He slowed his breathing and wiped his cheeks with the backs of his hands. "It's my ears."

"Your ears?" Pablo repeated.

Henry sighed and hung his head. "Yeah," he replied. "They bother me a lot. It always seems like people are yelling at me. Or telling me what to do. Sometimes I get lost in all the words when people talk.

So I just stop listening. When the noise is too much, I get nervous. And sometimes . . . I lose control."

Violet rested her hand on Henry's shoulder. "Why didn't you tell us?" she asked.

"I don't like to talk about it," Henry replied. He tugged on his costume. "I don't like being different from other kids. My moms say there isn't anything wrong with being different, but they don't understand."

"I know what it's like to be different," said Pablo. "When I first got to Newburg from Puerto Rico, it was really hard. I didn't speak English, and no one could understand me. It was easier once I made a friend," he said, smiling at Violet.

Henry lowered his eyes. "I don't really have friends. Well, I have one. A lady named Ms. Robinson comes to my house once a week. She said my ears are sensitive because I have auditory processing disorder. We do a lot of fun activities. My mama says they exercise my listening muscles. It's hard sometimes. But my mom says she's really proud of me. I don't know. I guess I still feel embarrassed about it."

Dr. Crisp knelt down in front of Henry. "The Maker Maze is for *everyone*, Henry. And there's no need to be embarrassed about something that makes you different. Our differences are what make us special."

Then Dr. Crisp pressed a button on her watch and whispered, "Maker Maze, activate sensory mode!"

The ground vibrated lightly.

boom snap whiz zap

Henry's face brightened. "Hey! That wasn't so bad!" he said.

"I should have turned on sensory mode sooner," said Dr. Crisp. "Henry, I'm sorry I didn't make the Maze more welcoming for you." She held out the Maker Manual.

"Maybe the Maze knew I also had a few things to learn today." She smiled.

"My dad always says you're never too old to learn something new," added Violet.

"I'm not *that* old!" replied Dr. Crisp. They all laughed.

"I'm really sorry I hurt your ears with the gong," Pablo said to Henry. "I should've been more patient."

Henry smiled. "Thanks, that really means a lot to me," he said. The two Makers reached up and gave each other a high five.

With his arm still in the air, Pablo noticed the time on his watch. "We only have thirty-five

Maker Minutes left! And we haven't even finished level two," he said.

"Flaming funnels!" said Dr. Crisp. "You better hurry!"

The trio huddled. "Let's think," said Violet. "When Pablo hit the gong, the jelly beans started bouncing."

"It's like the sound moved them," added Henry.

"But how?" Pablo asked.

"Maybe it was the plastic!" Violet bit her lip as she thought. "At our family cookout last summer, my cousin turned up the music really loud. The adults got so mad at him." She laughed.

"Violet! We have to focus!" said Pablo, tapping his watch.

"I know! Just listen. With the music so loud, the speaker started vibrating. I could see it shake!"

"So you think the sound made the plastic vibrate?" asked Henry.

"Yes! And that's what made the jelly beans move," replied Violet.

Pablo scratched his cheek. "That means sound makes our eardrum vibrate. And that's how we hear!" said Pablo.

RING, DING, DONG!

The Maker Maze jingle sounded softly. Pablo, Violet, and Henry cheered.

"You solved that one like science super-*hear*oes!" said Dr. Crisp as she handed out high fives.

"My dad said there's no sound in space," said Pablo. "Is that true?"

"It's kind of true," said Dr. Crisp. "Sounds travel like a wave through the air. And in order to make our eardrum vibrate, sounds have to make the air vibrate. But there's no air in space, so it's really hard to hear anything. That's why astronauts have fancy equipment to record space sounds! Space sounds are special, and we'd never be able to hear them by ourselves."

Then Dr. Crisp grabbed the Maker Manual. The book snapped open. The page read:

LEVEL 3: TARGET PRACTICE

Swipe up.

Dr. Crisp tapped her watch three times and quickly swiped up. A gust of wind blew up from the floor, sending Dr. Crisp's wild rainbow hair into the air. The bowl, jelly beans, and gong slid away.

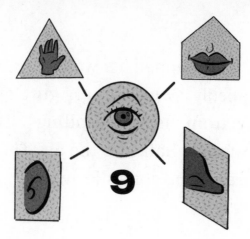

The Makers and Dr. Crisp were again standing in an empty room. Across from them were three targets. The center of each target was colored purple, with a black *M* drawn in the middle. The circle around the purple center was yellow, and the outer circle was neon blue.

"Okay, Makers. This is your final level. And it's all about sight!" said Dr. Crisp, rolling her eyes in opposite directions.

Henry's mouth fell open. "How did you do that?" he asked.

"It's one of my *many* secret talents," she said as she walked toward the targets. "As I'm sure you've noticed, we all have two eyes." Dr. Crisp spun around to face the Makers. "But why?" she asked with her hands in the air.

"Because we'd look like aliens if we only had one!" Pablo said jokingly. Violet and Henry giggled.

"Good guess!" Dr. Crisp winked. "But in this level, you're going to figure out the correct answer."

Dr. Crisp stuck her fingers in her mouth and whistled. A door in the corner of the room swung open, and three robots zoomed out. They sped over to the

Makers. They were each holding a drone and a controller.

"Oh, cool!" said Pablo as he took the drone from a robot's claw.

"These are like the ones in the Science Space at school!" said Violet.

"But even better!" added Henry. Every drone had a shiny black body with silver propeller blades attached to each of the four purple arms.

"Listen up!" began Dr. Crisp. "You are all going to stand here and wear one of these." She pulled three black eye patches out of her lab coat pocket and tossed one to each Maker. Violet stretched hers over her curls and fixed it into place.

"You look like a pirate," said Pablo, laughing as he put his on.

"Violet the pirate!" added Henry.

"Shiver me timbers!" said Violet in her best pirate voice.

"In this challenge, you will use the controller to fly the drone over the target in front of you," explained Dr. Crisp. She showed them the different buttons they needed to use to make the drone fly. "When you think the drone is hovering over the purple center of the target, press this button and a laser will blast out."

"Got it!" replied the Makers.

"You'll each try once with the eye patch and once without," continued Dr. Crisp. "Based on the results, you will have to decide why we use two eyes to see." She started rolling her eyes again.

Pablo, Violet, and Henry laughed.

Dr. Crisp raised both hands overhead. "Ready, set—"

"Wait!" Henry interrupted. He pulled on his costume sleeve. "I just want to make sure I got it." He pointed to a button on his controller. "This is the one I press for the laser, right?"

Dr. Crisp smiled with her arms in the air. "That's the one!"

Henry relaxed his shoulders and nodded to Dr. Crisp. "Okay, I'm ready."

Dr. Crisp lowered her arms quickly.

"Launch!"

The Makers sent their drones whizzing through the air. After making some adjustments, Violet blasted her laser over the target.

bizzap!

The yellow circle glowed.

"No way! I was right over the purple circle," Violet said with her hands on her hips.

Pablo's tongue stuck out of his mouth as he carefully positioned his drone.

bizzap!

The blue circle glowed!

"What?" he said. "Impossible!"

bizzap!

The yellow circle on Henry's target lit up.

"This makes no sense at all," said Pablo as he landed his drone on the floor. He took off his eye patch. "My drone was right above the middle of the target!"

"Mine too!" said Violet.

"Eye patches off!" said Dr. Crisp.

"Everything looks the same," said Henry as he snapped the patch off.

"Here goes nothing," said Pablo. He sent his drone flying into the air. Then

he very carefully positioned the drone and pressed the laser button on his controller.

bizzap!

The purple circle glowed.

"Yes!" Pablo said as he jumped into the air.

bizzap!

The centers of Violet's and Henry's targets glowed as well. But before the

Makers could celebrate, Dr. Crisp's watch started flashing.

"Muffling microscopes!" said Dr. Crisp.

"What's going on?" asked Henry.

"This isn't good," said Pablo. He swallowed hard.

"Oh no!" said Violet. "We're never going to make it!"

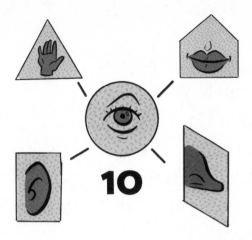

The Makers only had three minutes left to finish the level. Not to mention go back through the portal and get to the museum before their classmates unfroze!

"We have to think fast," said Violet. She bit her lip.

"Well, it was way easier using two eyes instead of one," said Henry.

"Yeah, with one eye I swore the drone was in the right spot," said Violet. "Even though it wasn't."

Henry tugged on his sleeve. "When we

had the patches on, we could still *see* the center of the target."

"But it was hard to know if the drone was actually over it or not," added Pablo.

"Maybe having two eyes helps us tell the *exact* location of things around us," said Henry.

RING, DING, DONG!

"Thank goodness!" said Pablo.

"Excellent work, Makers! But there's no time to celebrate. Thirty seconds left!" said Dr. Crisp. "Let's *see* our way out of here!" She tapped her watch three times and swiped down. The room with the model eardrum and gong flew into view. Then she swiped right, and the Makers were back onstage with the Mystery Maker Box.

"This way!" said Dr. Crisp. She ran off the stage, pushing a giant dog balloon out of her way.

POP!

Confetti exploded into the air.

Henry grabbed his ears.

"Sorry, Henry!" Dr. Crisp said over her shoulder.

Pablo, Violet, and Henry hurried behind. They made it to door number one and ran into the main lab of the Maker Maze.

The purple circle of light was starting to fade on the ceiling.

"Five seconds!" called Dr. Crisp. "Hurry and jump!"

The Makers ran as fast as they could toward the portal. They grabbed hands and leaped.

boom snap whiz zap

The portal closed.

The Makers tumbled through the giant nose onto the floor of the City Science Museum just as their classmates unfroze. A buzz of excited voices filled the lobby.

Pablo, Violet, and Henry stood up.

"We barely made it," said Pablo, trying to catch his breath.

"I know," said Violet. "I think I felt the portal pinch my toe!"

Then Henry faced his two new friends. "Thank you for taking me to the Maker Maze," he said. He tugged on his sleeve. "It really made me feel special."

The Makers hugged.

Henry noticed Mr. Eng walking their way. "Act normal," he said.

"What's that in his hair?" whispered Violet. "It looks like . . ."

"Confetti?" said Pablo. He scratched his cheek. "Can't be."

WORLD OF
§§§ SMELL §§§

"I'm glad to see you are all having a good time," said Mr. Eng.

"We're having a blast!" said Violet.

Pablo put his arms around Violet and Henry. "You know what, Mr. Eng? Field trip buddies are like eyes."

"Oh really?" said Mr. Eng with raised eyebrows. "How so?"

"Two are better than one!"

Make your own creations!

⋝MAKE A MODEL EARDRUM!⋜

Always *make* carefully and with adult supervision!

MATERIALS

1   rubber band
1   teaspoon of uncooked rice
        (about 25 grains)
    baking sheet
    bowl
    plastic wrap
    scissors
    wooden spoon

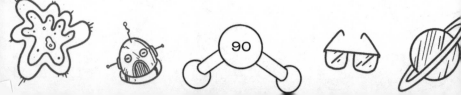

INSTRUCTIONS

1. Use scissors to carefully cut a piece of plastic wrap that is big enough to cover the bowl.

2. Stretch the plastic wrap over the bowl. Make sure it's stretched tightly! Secure it in place with a rubber band.

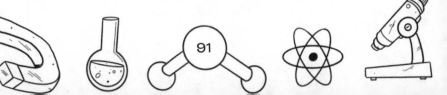

3. Spread one teaspoon of uncooked rice over the plastic.

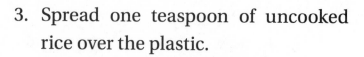

4. Make noise! Hit a baking sheet with a wooden spoon.
5. Watch the rice dance!

6. Try different types of noise. You can play loud music, yell, or clap your hands. Get creative!

7. Now think! Make observations about which sounds were able to move the rice.* You can also replace rice with sugar, small pieces of paper, or even jelly beans! Discuss your ideas with friends or family!

* You can create your own experiment sheet or ask your parent or guardian to download one at theannegriffith.com.

Your parent or guardian can share pictures and videos of your model eardrum on social medial using #MagnificentMakers.

⩾MAKE SCRATCH-AND-SNIFF CARDS!⩽

MATERIALS

3–4 different flavors of
     powdered Jell-O®
3–4 small plastic containers
     large white index cards
        (5" x 8")
     plastic cookie cutters
     white school glue

INSTRUCTIONS

1. Open the Jell-O packets and pour each into a separate small plastic container.

2. Put each cookie cutter on an index card. You might even be able to fit a few cookie cutters on one card.

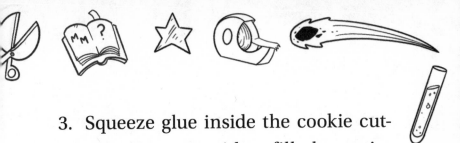

3. Squeeze glue inside the cookie cutters. You can either fill the entire cookie cutter or make an outline. It's up to you!*

* You can also paint freehand with the glue! You can even draw your name!

4. Sprinkle enough Jell-O powder to completely cover the glue. Get creative! You can use a different flavor for each cookie cutter or mix flavors! What happens to the Jell-O when it gets wet from the glue?

5. When you're done, remove the cookie cutters and let the glue dry overnight.
6. In the morning, carefully wipe away any extra powder from your cards.

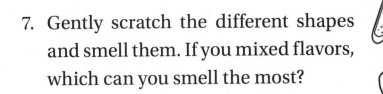

7. Gently scratch the different shapes and smell them. If you mixed flavors, which can you smell the most?

Your parent or guardian can share pictures and videos of your scratch-and-sniff cards on social media using #MagnificentMakers.

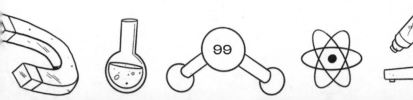

Acknowledgments

Jorge, thank you for encouraging me to chase my dreams. Your excitement about my writing journey is so motivating. Thank you, Dad, for introducing me to the joy of losing yourself in a good book. Mom, I miss you so much and wish more than anything you were physically here with me to enjoy this adventure. But I know that you're proud. Violeta and Lila, I started writing again because of you. I wanted kids like you to see themselves going on fun and exciting science adventures. I love you both so much. Many thanks, Kate, for your feedback on creating an authentic neurodiverse character. Stephanie, thank you for letting me bounce around weird ideas during our morning commute phone calls. It really helps get my creative juices flowing! Thank you to my wonderful agent, Liza Fleissig. You rock! Finally, I am grateful for the opportunity to work with such an amazing editor, Caroline Abbey, as well as the entire Random House team. Thank you for your continued guidance and support.

Can't get enough of
The Magnificent Makers?

Don't miss any of their adventures!

New friends. New adventures.
Find a new series . . . just for you!

For ballerina and fairy and vampire lovers

For adventurers

For unicorn lovers

For dog lovers

For mermaid and cat lovers

For sports fans

RHCB rhcbooks.com